Woody

The Kentucky Wiener

The Adoption

by
Leigh Anne Florence

Illustrations by James Asher

International Standard Book Number 0-9741417-0-4
Library of Congress Card Catalog Number 2003106482

Cover design by Asher Graphics
Book layout by ALC
Illustrations by James Asher

Manufactured in the United States of America

All book order correspondence should be addressed to:

HotDiggetyDog Press
P.O. Box 747
Shepherdsville, KY 40165

502-543-5315
leighanne@thewoodybooks.com
www.thewoodybooks.com

This book is dedicated
in loving memory
of my dad and fellow dog lover

Lonnie C. Furr
1924-1999

Special Thanks

As always, first and foremost to my husband, Ron. There is not enough ink or paper to describe what you mean to me. Thank you for everything. I love you! Always.

To Mama, Caroline, Patrick, Alex, and Preston. Love you all!

And finally, to my sweet, sweet puppies - Chloe and Woody. Thank you for bringing joy to my life every single day. I love seeing the world through your innocent eyes!

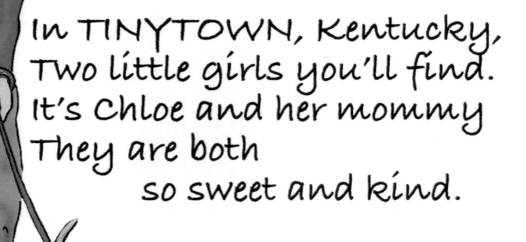

In TINYTOWN, Kentucky,
Two little girls you'll find.
It's Chloe and her mommy
They are both
        so sweet and kind.

They are very thankful
for their happy little home.
They spend their time together
They are never all alone.

For years it's just the two of them
They like it best that way.
They do all the great"girl" stuff
Like giggle, shop, and play.

"Mommy, I've been thinking
And it's really not so fair.
We have so much to offer
So I think that we should share.

If you stop and ponder,
I know you will agree
It's time we turn our duo
To a family of three.

I know you understand, Mommy
cause it's always been our goal
To give our hearts to others
And help the needy souls."

"Oh, my sweet, sweet Chloe
You're such a loving child!
How did you get so generous,
Well-mannered, meek, and mild?"

"We'll fill our home with love
And we will not hesitate.
It will bring us so much joy
To have a new playmate."

"We'll get up in the morning
While it's early and it's bright.
We'll drive out to the country
To find a pup that's right."

When it came the morning
They drove for many miles.
When they finally reach the country
Both their faces were all smiles.

Chloe couldn't believe it
When her four paws hit the ground-
Everywhere she looked
There were puppies all around.

"Look at all the wiener dogs!
Their bodies all so long!
I know I have to pick one
But I don't want to be wrong."

"Take your time now, Chloe!
Remember your good deed
To find that special puppy
Who looks like he's in need."

At that exact next moment
Coming from the back
Was a crying, lonely boy
Who was little, tan, and black.

"That's the one Mommy!
In my heart I know for sure.
He looks so sad and worried
Our home will be his cure."

we must name him, Mommy
To help take away his gloom.
Let's name him 'Mr. Dogwood'
Since the trees are full in bloom.

"Hey, little fellow,
Woody, if you will,
We're taking you back home now
To our house upon the hill."

"You are now our family
We're here in all you do!
We'll laugh and play
            and talk and share
Remember, we love you!"

Woody felt so blessed
And the girls could clearly see

That the home they had with two
was now much happier with three.